SOUL TO SOUL

SOUL TO SOUL

TINY STORIES OF HOPE AND RESILIENCE

Faye Rapoport DesPres

Published by Huntsville Independent Press
2112 Morningside Drive NW, Huntsville, AL 35810

For information about special discounts for bulk purchases, please contact Huntsville Independent Press at +1 (256) 678-0411 or Editor@ Huntsvilleindependent.com.

Huntsville Independent Press can bring authors to your live event.

For more information or to book an event, contact Huntsville Independent Press at +1 (256) 678-0411 or visit our website at www. HuntsvilleIndependent.com.

Also available in a HIP hardcover edition

Cover design by Anya Lauchlan
Interior design by HMDPUBLISHING

The text for this book was set in Garamond.

Manufactured in the United States of America
First HIP paperback edition December 2023

1 2 3 4 5 6 7 8 9 10

The Library of Congress has cataloged the hardcover edition as follows:

Names: DesPres, Faye, author.
Title: Soul to Soul: Tiny Stories of Hope and Resilience

Identifiers: LCCN (2023945496) ISBN 9798218269166 (pbk)

ISBN 9798218269173 (eBook) | ISBN 9798218270599 (hc)

To Jean-Paul

Every day with you is a tiny story.

Contents

Introduction

Dear reader, you might ask: "After years of writing stories containing 1000, 2000, 5000 words or more, why did you write one hundred 100-word stories?"

The answer is both simple and not-so-simple (as are the stories).

It started with a writing exercise I took part in with a friend. To nudge ourselves to write daily (a habit I'd gotten away from), we each committed to writing at least 100 words per day. Those words could be in any form—a paragraph from a personal essay or story, a re-write of part of a piece we were working on…anything. The only goal was to write at least 100 words.

As a writer, I do well with goals and structure. The exercise inspired me to return to a daily writing practice. Interestingly, from the start, I began crafting complete stories in 100 words. I didn't start out with that intention. The first time I did it, I thought it was a lark. Somehow, I got hooked.

Before I knew it, every morning I was writing a 100-word story. A few were inspired by news stories or events in my own life (although I always fictionalized details and other aspects of the stories). Most came completely from my imagination.

My own worldview began to emerge as one story followed another, each developing its own shape and purpose. Somehow by writing these tiny fictional stories, I found myself crafting a form of my own story—not my *actual* story, but the story of my soul.

A bit of research revealed that I am far from the first writer to work with 100-word stories. Flash fiction, of course, has been popular for some time, but usually flash fiction contains more than 100 words. I discovered that there is an actual term for 100-word stories. They're called "drabbles." There are even literary journals devoted to the form (a few of them published some of the stories in this book).

Writing a complete story in 100 words isn't easy. It presents quite a challenge to the writer. It's a bit like putting the pieces of a puzzle together, but instead of puzzle pieces, the writer is fitting words together to create a picture, a picture that also has meaning. I found the process to be both challenging and fun.

There's one last thing. If you've read my first book, a memoir-in-essays titled *Message From a Blue Jay*, you know I've faced some challenges (who hasn't). When *Message From a Blue Jay* was published, many readers wrote to say they felt less alone after reading it. It was comforting to learn that someone else had gone through something similar to their own experience.

A few readers, however, felt the book was too sad. Some even used the word "depressing." I never intended for *Message From a Blue Jay* to be depressing. I tried to balance any sadness with revelations of understanding—and I thought I'd ended the book on a positive and hopeful (perhaps even funny) note.

Partly as a reaction to those responses, my next three books were children's books. Each book in the Stray Cat

Stories series is designed to delight young readers with a hopeful story about a real-life rescued cat who found his or her happy ending.

Now, we arrive at this book. When I wrote these tiny stories, I decided from the start that I wanted to offer something positive and hopeful for adult readers. I wanted readers to be able to pick up this book and get a little boost, whether they were feeling happy or sad. During a period of time when our world is struggling, I wanted to focus on some of the positive and redeeming qualities of the human spirit, such as hopefulness, resilience, and creativity.

So, dear reader, I hope these stories will make you smile. I hope they'll make you stop and think, "There *is* good in the world."

That hope is my gift to you, soul to soul.
- Faye

PART

One:

PERSISTENCE

Ninth Inning

Despite the warm day, Cal felt cold. His hands shook as he attempted to grip the baseball bat.

The pitcher stared straight into Cal's eyes, his fingers fiddling with the ball behind his back.

Cal swallowed. His coach wasn't even watching. A few of his teammates were packing up their gear.

Strike one!

Parents on the bleachers stood, stretched, and headed for the stairs.

Strike two!

Cal glanced at his father, still sitting in his seat, smiling and shaking his fist in encouragement.

Cal's eyes returned to the pitcher. He took a deep breath. The ball flew towards him.

Crack.

Darkness

The dawn was drab, and George's old boots were caked with mud. He was weary from a night of work; he felt the dirt lodged between his fingernails and skin. He walked the quiet streets, pulling at the collar of a worn wool coat.

A small boy knelt before a shack of a house, dressed in hand-me-downs. His toes poked through shoes with ragged holes. He was pushing a rock through a puddle.

"What are you doing?" George asked curiously.

The boy looked up, dark eyes shining in the gleam of the streetlight.

"I am building a castle," he said.

By the Sea

She couldn't deny who and what she was. Still, their admonitions echoed in her head until it hurt.

"You must be practical."

"Why not try law school?"

"How about a career in nursing?"

The pale sky hung above the rolling waves. A lone seagull floated in circles on the breeze, its backdrop blue with wisps of cloud.

She understood their concerns, of course. She'd probably be waiting tables or cleaning bathrooms for years. The life she wanted would be hard, full of rejection.

Yet even on the beach—without paint—she found herself drawing with a stick in the sand.

No Way

She refused to let him go. They tried to convince her, but there was no way.

The night had been frigid, with snow falling hard. Harsh, heavy winds had whistled through the woods. She'd been close to giving up. The cold, loneliness, and fear had engulfed her.

He'd found her sitting in the middle of a field and stayed until the snow stopped. She wrapped her arms around his neck; his body warmed her.

When they found her, she was still holding on.

There was no way she'd let them take the dog to the pound. Not now, not ever.

Persistence

"I give up," she cried out, tired and frustrated.

Seeing her despair, he grabbed his coat.

"Follow me," he suggested.

They walked down the street to the park with the Little League field, where a teenage boy tossed a ball for a barking dog.

"Where are we going?" she asked.

He paused at the edge of the baseball field. Puzzled, she glanced around. He pointed. All she saw was a sad little stump, a small tree felled to make way for a new fence. Then she raised her eyebrows.

Leaves were sprouting from the stump.

"*Never* give up," he said.

Saved

All she wanted was to live. How confusing it had been to be taken from her home and encased in decoration. All for display.

Still, she thrived, growing tall and lean. She blossomed. People paused when they saw her, admiring.

Thankfully, her beauty touched someone's heart. That, or the way she continued to thrive despite declarations that she could not be saved.

What a relief it was when those hands removed the wax. They placed her gently into a pot of fresh dirt. Now she could breathe. Now she could be a real amaryllis, growing and blooming into the years.

Waiting

She lay on her back on the hard ground. Her ski jacket provided cushioning, and a pom-pom'ed knit hat cradled her head. Sunglasses shielded her eyes from the sun when it peeked through the clouds.

Tired of the city rush, she'd driven for miles to find solitude.

She lay there for a long time breathing the cold, crisp air. Waiting. She was determined; they'd promised it would happen.

After a while, she closed her eyes and fell asleep.

Thankfully, she didn't miss it. She awoke to the sensation and opened her eyes, smiling when the first flake hit her face.

This Work

Pulling a soiled cloth out of his pocket, he wiped his brow. The sun beat down relentlessly, making him ponder why he was chosen for this path.

Usually, he didn't wonder. He focused on the field, the task at hand. This work was his only option, though it strained his sore back. It had been his only option for years.

He couldn't know the future. He could only give it as a gift.

"I did it!" his son cried. He looked up. The young man was running towards him, waving a paper in his hand. "I'm in, Papa, I'm in!"

The Kitten

She was desperate; the kitten was sick. Back then, stray cats slinked through Israel's streets seeking food. She couldn't let this one suffer.

The night was cold, and the sky bloomed with stars. She dialed a friend back in the States whose husband was a veterinarian.

A woman knocked on the phone booth door. Recognizing her, she slid the door open and explained.

"May I pray for your kitten?" the woman asked gently.

"Of course," she replied.

Their religions were different, but what did that matter? She would take any prayer, any hope.

The kitten was fine the next morning.

空手道

Fighting Back

Something was wrong. Sensei didn't know what it was. The new student's body was clearly athletic, but she moved slowly, without strength.

Sensei demonstrated a defensive stance. Then he held up a pad and asked her to punch it. She hesitated, then struck without force.

Months would pass before he learned of her illness—the surgeries, depression, medications.

Watching her now, he had to rely on his instincts. Lifting the pad again, he said: "Pretend it's someone, or something, you're really mad at."

A spark lit in her exhausted eyes. Then she lifted her fists and punched—hard this time.

Pearls

It starts as a tiny irritation — a grain of sand or a parasite. It's the process that transforms it into a pearl that is unexpected.

Labeling the infiltrator an "intruder," the mollusk coats it with a material from within—layers of the same substance it uses to build its shell.

The mollusk produces layer upon layer of nacre, also known as "mother of pearl." This transforms what irritates or threatens the creature into something completely harmless. Not just something harmless, something beautiful.

It's a question to consider: can we do the same thing? How can *we* be mothers of pearls?

The Angel ICDI

Emma noticed the little girl crying in a driveway. A banana-seat bike lay next to her on its side.

"What's wrong?" Emma asked.

"I can't ride my new bike," the girl said.

"Have you asked the Angel ICDI to help? You pronounce it like 'Ick-dee'."

The girl stared at her, then took a deep breath. "Angel ICDI, will you help me?"

Then she stood, pulled the bike up, and threw one leg over the frame. "Help me, Angel ICDI," she asked again.

The girl started peddling and soon was riding in circles.

"I Can Do It!" she laughed.

Emma winked.

Wishing on a Star

On cloudy nights, she searched.

The rules were highly particular. The star had to be the first one she saw each evening; if she saw two at once, there would be no wish that night.

She had to stare at the star while saying, "Star light, star bright, first star...." Then she stated her wish.

If she stood on her toes, it would bring her closer to the star and to her wish.

Her mother watched, peeking through the half-closed bedroom doorway. She couldn't stay for long, though. The tiny puppy in her arms was wriggling, and it might whimper.

The Memories

She felt scared when people tried to get close. She wished she could explain what had happened, but she had no words.

The memories were dim, but they were always present, pictures in her mind. She could still see and sense where she had been.

Anyone displaying benevolence or love ended up disappointed.

One woman refused to give up. Day after day, she sat quietly nearby, showing nothing but kindness and respect. This woman gave her time and didn't push.

So, one day when the woman reached out, she stayed still. She let the woman pet her, and she purred.

The Mobile

One wooden fish had a bright yellow face, orange scales, and blue polka dots. Another had a painted pink rose on its side.

A rose on a fish? Why not?

In the middle, a round blowfish floated in the air, blue comb like a rooster's, mouth gaping. Their tails twisted gently when she opened the window.

Andrea refused to swim in the ocean after *Jaws*. Why risk it? No way. When friends tried to convince her to dive, she'd ask, *why?*

When she finally did dive, off Cozumel, she understood.

The mobile was her reminder to always ask: *why not?*

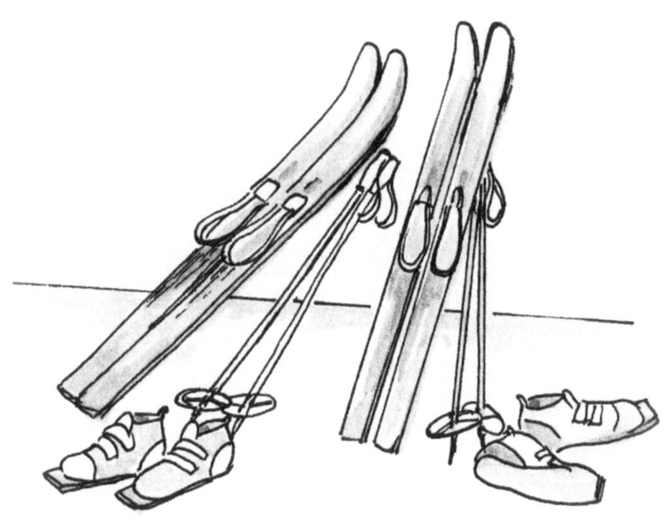

They Skied

The war began, so they skied.

People suffered and struggled for safety. When they turned on the TV, images of destruction assaulted their senses. He grew nervous; she became stressed. They both felt a thick, deep sadness.

What now?

He descended the stairs and retrieved their skis, poles, and boots from the basement. After carrying them up, he opened the front door. Crisp, cold air flew in.

They drove to the woods and carried the skis to the edge of a narrow trail. Then they skied and breathed as the snowflakes swirled, knowing the peace hidden there would survive us.

A Marriage

After thirty-five years, she didn't want to leave.

Memories trailed behind them like the train on her wedding dress: the wind whipping her hair on their honeymoon by the sea, an embrace in their first house, two dogs, three children. Now, a grandchild was on the way.

His words had cut deeply. They'd been arguing more, and she was tired. She set up an appointment for them both with a therapist.

Was there a right answer? A wrong one?

Where was the line between love and longing?

She didn't know. All she could do—at least first—was try love.

PART

Two:

INSPIRATION

Friends

Living alone was hard, but at night she touched base with her friends.

Elizabeth went on about her big romance, how it started off badly but had grown into a marriage that made her quite happy.

Anna's life was more depressing, but she listened because hearing about it touched her soul.

She still talked to Alice, though Alice was younger and had strange friends.

When she needed cheering up, there was Don. He was a bit of a crackpot, but he always made her smile.

That night it was Don, so she fell asleep smiling after turning the last page.

Coming Home

After such a long flight, he had no idea how his buddy would feel by the time he arrived at the gate. They had been inseparable overseas, serving together and comforting each other the way soldiers do, without words.

A year had passed. He hadn't known if his friend would survive, never mind if they would see each other again. When he got the phone call, he cried.

He dressed in fatigues to be sure he'd be visible in the crowd of applauding well-wishers.

He could have worn a clown suit. Once released, his buddy raced towards him, paws flying.

The Sea in October

Twelve-foot waves splashed against the side of the vessel. Ilana wished she had taken more medicine; she'd never done well on boats. The October sea was playing with this one like a hacky sack, kicking it up and down, back and forth.

"It will be worth it, Ilana," her friends had insisted.

"I'll never forget *that* advice," she thought ruefully. She felt cold, wet, and nauseous, even inside the cabin.

Urgent words suddenly crackled over the PA system. The passengers scrambled onto the deck. Ilana followed, grasping her stomach.

When the humpback whale leaped from the sea, she forgot everything.

The House

Each small detail was critical. The rug in the living room was soft, infused with color. The furniture was carefully planned and placed; each bedroom had a complete set, including oval mirrors.

Prints of the great masters hung on the walls. She even found copies of Georgia O'Keefe watercolors displaying blooming flowers.

Finally, the house looked just as she'd imagined. The final touch: space heaters for cold winter days in any room without a fireplace.

Then she called her parents and insisted they come see the house.

"Mom, Dad!"

She'd added dogs and cats to complete her miniature animal shelter.

Don't Be Late

He couldn't be late. After everything he'd been through—the frustration, the failure—he needed this.

When the alarm sounded, his first thought was to silence it. His second thought was: *Not today; don't be late.* So, he sat up and tossed the thick blanket off his body.

He dressed, brushed his teeth, and ran his hand through his hair. For a moment, he stared at his face in the mirror. Then he raced down the stairs and flung open the front door.

Stepping out onto the porch, he laughed because he'd made it. There it was: the beautiful sunrise.

Intended

They intended to get one dog. The decision was made after a family meeting; the children were thrilled.

"Will we adopt a shepherd?"

"A poodle!"

"Something tiny and yappy!"

They decided to visit the shelter and adopt whichever dog called out to them. The breed wouldn't matter. Mixed would be fine.

At the shelter, the children fell in love with Rocky. A sizable shepherd/husky mix, he was soft-eyed, gentle, and four years old.

They intended to get one dog, but Rocky glanced back at the skinny brown mutt he was leaving behind.

They looked at each other…and got two dogs.

Her Face

Josh didn't think it was a big deal. Some teasing in the hall, a taunt in the cafeteria.

They're just kids being kids, he told himself. He avoided looking at her face. Establishing himself in this school had taken time. He felt like he was "in," and he didn't want to mess that up.

One day, in the cafeteria, Josh glanced as he walked by. Her head was bowed; he could tell she was crying.

When the next barb came, something broke through his brain. Without thinking, he whipped around and yelled at them. "STOP!"

Looking up, her face changed.

Enrico

Enrico always waved when his neighbors returned. They would pause, set down their suitcases on the stone path, then visit with Enrico while he worked in his flower garden.

"How was the trip?" Enrico would ask.

"It was wonderful!" was the inevitable reply. They shared photos of the Eiffel Tower or tortoises in the Galapagos. Enrico marveled at the images.

Once, after sharing a picture of the Great Wall of China, the wife asked Enrico why he never traveled.

"There's a whole world in the six million acres of this state," Enrico explained. "I still haven't seen it all yet."

Soul to Soul

He would never be able to describe it. He didn't understand the fancy words, and he didn't have the money to take courses.

He borrowed some books from the library, and the books gave him a few ideas. He kept these ideas to himself. They'd scoff at him if he spoke and interrupted the guide who used the fancy words.

A soul out in the universe had asked a question, and he hoped that soul knew he heard it now.

He stared at the painting for a while longer before returning home. There, he answered the question with his brush.

The Artist

Judith worked in clay, oils, watercolors, and batik. A trained illustrator, she'd married young and had a son. After her divorce, she taught art in a local public school.

She bought a small fixer-upper house. Two portraits of her son hung in the living room. Massive batiks covered several walls. She pasted Van Gogh prints onto the kitchen cabinets and embellished them with oils. Clay busts sat on a windowsill.

"Why don't you sell your art?" a friend asked.

Judith shrugged. It was the creating that mattered. When she was gone, she wouldn't be remembered.

Unless someone wrote about her.

Check Mate

Steve enjoyed bragging about his prowess at chess. Whenever Abigail studied in the student lounge, he arrived with his chess set and challenged another student to play. He always won.

Steve only challenged boys; it was beneath him to believe a girl could win.

Abigail's father was born in Europe; he had taught her to play chess when she was four. Still, she remained silent, until the day Steve passed by and accidentally brushed her book off the table.

"Oh, sorry," he said, continuing on his way without picking up the book.

Abigail looked up.

"Shall we play?" she asked.

Xinyi

Like many of her friends, Xinyi played the viola. She'd been taking lessons since age four.

Her parents joked about having headaches and no peace. In the mornings, Xinyi lifted her bow before school. In the afternoons, her parents insisted she do homework first. At night, when Xinyi slept, her mother gently slipped the bow from her daughter's hand.

Xinyi smiled as she dreamed. The fingers on her left hand twitched.

By the time Xinyi was ten, her parents understood.

Like many of her friends, Xinyi played the viola. However, Xinyi, in her joy, would one day *play the viola.*

What Dancing is Like

She thought about the reporter's question. Finally, she spoke.

"Dancing is like a tree swaying to the music of the wind, or flower petals drifting across a summer field. It's like a bite of cake so delicious you close your eyes, or being lifted, weightless, up towards the sky."

She smiled, adding, "Dancing is like a glimpse of the person you love."

Several journalists nodded and jotted down notes, but one man shook his head and looked confused. She left the podium and reached for his hand.

He stood, and she spun him in circles until he laughed, finally understanding.

The Elephant

She'd always loved elephants. An elephant batik hung on her wall. A green ceramic elephant lamp sat on her desk.

The flight to the sanctuary in Tennessee took three hours, but she knew every long minute would be worth it.

When she arrived, a heavy rain was pelting the ground. But for her, nothing mattered except the truck slowly rolling through the gate. She had worked so hard raising money for this day.

The vehicle stopped, and two volunteers lowered a heavy ramp.

Then the elephant, white scars visible above his wide feet, took his first, halting steps towards freedom.

Clad in Socks

Liam spotted the man sitting on the curb, his feet clad in socks full of holes. After two more steps, Liam stopped and turned around. People pushed past them in a rush, pursuing whatever was so important.

Liam asked the man, "Are you alright?"

The man looked about sixty, but he could have been thirty with weather-worn cheeks and wisps of waxy hair. "Alright?" he responded, eyes blinking, confused.

The question, Liam realized, was absurd. He took off his shoes and handed them to the man. Then he helped him stand up and made a quick call, clad in socks.

The Trade-off

She was devastated, the way only teenagers can be. Her beloved cat had been missing for days.

Now she'd lost her favorite necklace. The metal wasn't precious; she'd purchased it at the five-and-dime. Still, the fake diamond that hung from the cheap chain sparkled.

To avoid getting a tan line around her neck, she had placed the necklace carefully in the grass near her towel before lying down to soak up some sun. When she stood up, the necklace was gone.

She searched and searched. Then she cried all night.

The next morning her cat wandered home, thin and hungry.

Crazy Cat Lady

The neighbors raised their eyebrows and sipped tea. "Why does Anna feed those cats?"

An organization had helped Anna install insulated cat houses and set up a feeding station. Each cat was trapped, neutered, and vaccinated. Those young enough to be tamed were adopted; the rest returned to live their lives.

One day, a neighbor approached Anna. "We'll have cats forever," she complained.

"I'm changing that," Anna explained. "As the cats age, the colony will diminish."

"Crazy cat lady," the neighbor muttered.

Anna didn't care. She hadn't been able to save her father, but she could save these little lives.

Dreams

Her midnight dreams used to come true. Reality was never exact, but it was close.

At age ten, she dreamed she had two horses. A week later, her visiting aunt presented a plastic bag. Inside were two horses: one plastic, one stuffed.

At thirty-three, she dreamed about meeting the bass player from a famous band. A month later, a bass player from a different band called to ask about an item sold in her family's store.

At fifty-five, she wondered where the magic had gone. Then her husband, once an impossible dream, limped in and kissed her on the cheek.

She Waited

Her mother had protected her for as long as possible, but one day she'd taken the leap. That day both scared and thrilled her.

Since then, her life had been uncertain. An anonymous friend found her a place to stay where she'd be safe and warm. Then she waited.

She waited for a good two weeks. Life was cold, dark, and quiet. Then the sun grew stronger, the weather warmed, and water fell from the sky.

One day, she could wait no longer. So, the young sunflower pushed out and up, rose from the ground, and grew her first leaf.

Trees

No trick she ever tried worked. For years she drove three hours back and forth, first between her hometown and the university, then after she moved into a home of her own. The highway got boring, so she created a special game: spot a tree on the way there, find it again on the way home.

She could never spot the same tree.

One day she was mowing the lawn for an elderly neighbor when he stepped outside to chat. She told him about the trees.

He thought for a moment and said, "Believe your eyes, or trust the trees."

PART
Three:
REALIZATIONS

The Woods

She was frustrated, so she drove to the wildlife sanctuary and followed a trail into the woods.

Snow had fallen, and icicles dripped from the trees. A woodpecker chirped.

What is the point of my life? she wondered. *I get up, go to work, do it again.*

She walked for a while, hands in her pockets, breathing crisp air.

The crack of a branch on the ground nearby stopped her. She froze, then turned.

A doe stood among the trees. For a moment, they stared at each other. Then the doe trotted off.

Awe-struck, she understood. *This is the point.*

She Wondered

Fifty years had passed since it happened. The dock was worn and weathered. She sat carefully, removed her sandals, and dipped her toes in the cool water.

The sun glared at her. The lake offered relief, as it always had.

Voices echoed through the woods and over the water. They were only in her mind: children laughing, counselors instructing kids learning to canoe.

Often, she'd wondered if her life had any meaning. But she had saved a child here, leaping into the water as he struggled.

Two days ago she read that he, now a doctor, had discovered the cure.

The Giver

It started with gummies. Her mother placed a bag inside her lunch box every day. She gave them all away, hoping the other kids would like her.

In high school, she had a crush on a cute boy. She gave him the best seat, and then she couldn't see.

Away at university, she baked lemon cakes. She gave all the slices to students who studied in the lounge late at night.

One day after work, she paused at a window and stared. People on the sidewalk bustled behind her.

She stepped into the bakery, bought lemon cake, and ate it.

Skating

Every day at noon she warmed her lunch in the microwave. On the walk back to her desk, she paused at the window. Her cubicle had no windows.

The children were always there, wrapped in coats, scarves, and hats with pom-poms. They skated around the snow-cleared rectangle, sliding back and forth or in circles around the pond. She imagined their shrill shrieks, their laughter.

Then she returned to her desk, opened the plastic container, and stared at the leftovers from last night's take-out.

One evening, she found her old skates in a dusty box. The next day, she brought them.

Press, Swipe, Press

Where was that text? Flicking through threads of words on her phone, she scrolled until she found that message she remembered. She read it again and smiled.

Considering it for a moment, she decided to respond. Click-clicking quickly, her thumbs flew back and forth, finding the perfect places to press.

She stared down at her device, waiting. Had Fiona forgotten her phone? Anxiety crept in. Then a notification nudged her to check her email.

Press, swipe, press: just an ad from the pharmacy.

Lola's leash tugged at her hand.

Suddenly she looked up, remembering her dog and the setting sun.

Holiday Hassles

What a frustrating season so far! December had been rainy. Where was the snow? The holidays were almost here, but it hardly felt festive.

So many tasks remained unfinished. She had to shop for more presents, wrap them, then find someplace to store them where the kids wouldn't look.

What would she wear to the party on Friday? She needed ingredients for the gingerbread cookies!

She was finishing her power walk, completing the day's steps, when the sight of him stopped her.

He was making his bed, laying a torn blanket over old, worn-out pillows next to a shopping cart.

Superman

The boys at school teased him relentlessly when he insisted his grandfather was Superman.

"Sure, he is!"

"Your grandfather's the janitor!"

"I never saw Superman clean toilets before!"

The grandfather didn't know; he spent his days wiping countertops and mopping hallway floors. He always greeted students with a smile or a joke.

On "Show and Tell" day, one student brought a coin collection, another a quartz rock, another *Let It Bleed* from 1969.

The boys fell silent when he walked in with his grandfather, who showed his Silver Star. He wore his uniform from the Vietnam War. It still fit.

Gone

He didn't understand. She was sobbing again at the bottom of the stairs, but this time she smiled while the tears fell.

"What is it?" he asked.

She shook her head, unable to answer. Finally, she took a deep breath and replied, "You won't believe me."

He waited.

"For years, every time I came downstairs, I saw her pink ball in the middle of the rug. She used to play with it at night."

"Honey, her toys are gone. She's been gone for eight weeks."

"But look!" she said, pointing at the rug. In the middle sat the pink ball.

The Golden Swan

The swan globe was a gift. Encased in water and golden snowflakes, the swan, lit up, spun slowly in circles. No music, just beauty in a dark room.

One morning after dusting the globe, she placed it back on the shelf. When she turned around, it fell off the edge.

Gold spread across the floor in a pool of water. She cried. He could not console her.

He drove forty-five minutes to the store and bought another one.

At first, she thought, *it's not the same*. Then, seeing the hope in his eyes, she changed her mind.

Yes, it is.

Red Planet

Arlen swore he saw a bright red planet. Not Mars, because Mars wasn't located there, but when he lay in his bed staring up through the skylight, he saw it, clear as night.

His mother stood near the bed staring upwards. She couldn't see it.

His father peered in the direction where he pointed. No luck there, either.

Only Arlen could see his red planet. So, he named it "Planet Arlen," and he loved it.

(Tell me, what makes Planet Arlen less real than other planets? Not the red light on the power strip on the floor, that's for sure).

Seeing

She had never seen anything like this bird.

It wasn't large or small. Bright orange eyes matched a long, narrow beak; its black body boasted a white breast. The bird hopped among the rocks near the hotel's driveway.

She marveled at the sight, thinking, *this bird must be common to someone who lives here, but to me it is enchanting.* She took photos.

Once home, she stepped out back to sit under the umbrella. A flock of house sparrows flitted between the branches of the pine tree.

Sparrows—so familiar. Now she watched them, seeing them for the first time.

Young Faces

She started seeing young faces in elderly ones.

It began when her 80-year-old father propped himself up onto the motorcycle he could no longer ride. "I see myself so differently than the world sees me," he sighed. A wistful expression flitted across his face and fading eyes.

The words he spoke that day never left her. In the mirror, she saw a girl in her middle-aged face. On the streets, it happened everywhere. Wrinkles disappeared from deeply lined faces. Every smile, even toothless, radiated robust youth.

Time does its thing. The mind is the only tool that can defeat it.

Something They Needed

She felt bored. Every day was much the same; her husband left for work, she sweated on the exercise bike, the kids texted from their ivory league dorms (usually about something they needed). Maria arrived to clean at 10.

Sometimes she wished she hadn't given up criminal law; at least she'd had something to do.

Eight miles away, her sister raised the blinds at the youth center. "Will Eddie be in today?" she asked a volunteer.

"I hope so; his mom was arrested last night."

"Oh, no. She was doing so well."

"We need a good lawyer," the volunteer sighed.

The Lead Singer

Ally won tickets and VIP passes in the company lottery. Now, she and Ruth sat just feet from the stage.

She'd always felt a connection to this band. Every song mirrored a moment in her life. In her dreams, she had long conversations with the lead singer, as if they were close friends.

After the show, they were ushered backstage. The drummer walked by; then they saw the lead singer. Ally caught his eye, and he smiled. But she tugged Ruth's sleeve, and giggling like teenagers, they left.

Somehow Ally knew that certain things are meant to remain in dreams.

The Place

She had come for a kind of closure, but now she wasn't sure if such a thing was ever possible.

This was the place where those who came before her had suffered. She could hear their cries and see the fear in their eyes.

The wind whistled through the trees and touched her hair. For a while she stood quietly with an ache in her gut. Tears trickled down her cheeks.

Finally, he took her hand, and she looked at him.

She was here, after all, despite what had happened. She was here. There was love. And that was all.

The Audience

Some said the audience was what mattered—after the music, of course. He agreed.

When he was four, his parents gave him a toy guitar. He played it so much that they purchased a real one and arranged for some lessons. The teacher's eyebrows lifted when he heard the boy play.

Since then, he'd done it all: world tours, private jets, the Grammy Awards.

Now, every Sunday, he drove to a small venue outside town. No roadies, not even any money from the door—just a musician and his attentive audience.

Lined up by the fence to listen, they moo-ed.

Happy As He Was

He was afraid his woolen hat would fall off, but it didn't. He didn't mind cold winter mornings. They offered such jolts of joy.

His memories were scant, but the ones he had were all pleasant. He certainly loved his children. They ran to him every afternoon, hugging him tight and patting his stomach. He wished he could join them when they wrapped their hands around steaming mugs of hot chocolate, but of course that wouldn't be good for him.

So, he remained happy as he was, standing in the front yard waving jauntily at passers-by with his stick arms.

The Disagreement

They sat together at lunchtime, disagreeing.

"I think…" she said.

"I disagree," he replied.

The disagreement got heated.

"I believe…" he asserted.

"But…" she responded.

Their opposition grew, then spread into tributaries like water flowing from a high mountain snowpack.

The problem came when he said, "You are…!"

Angry, she answered, "No, *you* are!"

They stopped speaking. In silence, they swallowed the final bites of their sandwiches and drank the last drops of their drinks.

He reached out his hand. After a moment, she took it.

"You are not…" he said.

"Neither are you," she responded.

They went back inside.

PART
Four:
RESILIENCE

Contraband

Darkness pressed against his skin in the narrow alley. He glanced around nervously, queasy from the acrid smell of the dumpster.

The cash in his pocket felt damp from his sweaty grip.

A figure appeared, silhouetted in light from a lamp above the street. High heels clicked, echoing as the figure approached.

He swallowed hard.

"Do you have it?" he whispered.

He couldn't see the face hidden beneath the hood, but the woman nodded and held out a package. She took the money.

At home, he drew the curtains and ripped the package open. There it was: the banned book.

The Blinds

Olivia stared at the window blinds. She'd bought them when she moved into the apartment after the messy divorce. Their cream color perfectly matched the cornice molding and the casing around the windows.

At night she shut the window blinds tight, and in the mornings, she only let in necessary light—nothing that might shock the interior. She adjusted the blinds as the sun moved across the sky, always maintaining a certain amount of shadow.

It had been a year now. Olivia stared at the blinds.

Then, with a tug, she pulled them up completely, letting bright sunlight stream in.

Party Clown

The jokes did not stop. He'd been like this since child-hood, constantly cracking up his classmates. Often his teachers had to hide their smiles as they sent him off to the principal.

His rapid-fire words made the partygoers laugh, buckle over, even cringe. He played off their energy, off every grin he got, every face that fell out of a polite party pose.

When the clock struck midnight and the champagne bottles popped, she noticed he wasn't in the room.

Hallway? No. Kitchen, not there either.

She found him outside staring at the moon. Touching his shoulder, she glimpsed tears.

A Cardinal

She was better now that a year had passed, but Valentine's Day prompted a pang of painful missing. Each year he'd burst through the front door carrying roses. The card always featured a cardinal whose bright red feathers matched the flowers.

Now that he was gone, she dreaded this day. She tried to sleep late, but eventually she couldn't stay in bed any longer.

The house felt empty, so she opened the front door and stepped outside.

A cardinal was perched on the burlap bag covering their rose bush. She smiled, just slightly.

Beneath the burlap, new buds were forming.

Their Old House

She smiled with a tinge of sadness. It was hard to visit their old house. The front door was still the same fire-engine red; pink roses still blossomed in the flower bed.

Across the street in her car, she reminisced. Dayna was ten when they planted those roses. Paddy Puppy was still an actual pup.

The front door opened. Two toddlers, probably twins, waddled outside excitedly. Following, a woman carried small pails and matching shovels in her overloaded arms. The group walked towards the flower bed, where plastic pots of perennials waited to be planted.

The sadness left her smile.

Up the Mountain

Angus would make it, but a medal was out of reach. The steep mountain race wasn't the hardest he'd done; two years ago, he would have won easily. Now, it was a challenge.

Everything since the accident was a challenge.

The finish line was near. Three cyclists rode ahead. He would finish off the podium, but he'd finish. Fourth place was an achievement—especially after everything he'd been through.

Hiroshi, in third place, glanced back.

Don't worry, I'm no threat, Angus thought.

When Hiroshi slowed down to let him pass, something more than sweat dampened the scar on his face.

Generations

The year had been difficult. Looking back, it was hard to find something good. He'd lost his job, and now they could lose the house.

His father's face haunted him. That gravelly voice.

"What a joke."

"You're a failure."

"The dog could do better than you." Usually he'd been drunk, his eyes bloodshot, face red.

Little Billy tottered into the doorway. "Dadda!" he called, teetering halfway across the room before falling. The boy started to cry.

He rushed over to Billy, picked him up, and kissed his head. "Don't cry," he said, cuddling his son. "Look how far you ran!"

The Last Gift

She hadn't slept since her father died. She'd sat by his hospital bed and begged him to stay, but after 86 years and all the pain, he'd had enough.

Now when she closed her eyes, she could see him on stage, bow flying across the strings on his violin. The orchestra was frantic behind him, the audience on its feet.

No lessons had made her play like that.

On Christmas, alone, she came downstairs. He'd set up a small tree for her before he collapsed, leaving a gift beneath it. Slowly, she unwrapped the box.

Inside was his shining violin.

Hemshil

His classmates were enjoying the school Olympics today, but not Hemshil. He was trapped at home, sick. No mat-pushing race for Hemshil. No balancing an egg on a spoon.

Hemshil stared at the ceiling. It was hot for late spring, and the ceiling fan whirred in circles, brushing his cheeks with a light breeze.

Hemshil imagined the breeze lifting him up. His sheet became a magic carpet, and he flew over the rooftops towards the schoolyard. He hovered above the races and cheered the other children.

His mother's voice interrupted. "How do you feel, Hemshil?"

Hemshil smiled. "I feel free."

The War

He remembered the war. Many had forgotten, but he had not.

Sometimes, at night, he was afraid to close his eyes. He might see fellow soldiers couched in cold ground, hear the rumbles and roars that shook broken buildings, the booms, the blasts, the discharged howls.

He might see the frightened eyes of stray dogs.

On those nights he sat up, listening to classical music and staring at the stars, so high above it all.

Standing at the door in those moments, her fingers felt the ghosts of shoulder sleeve insignias sewed during the war. Silently, they reached for him.

The Attic

It happened by accident.

A student abroad in Amsterdam, she rented an attic converted into an apartment. She'd find friends, learn a language, sample local life. Anyway, she loved Van Gogh and red tulips.

The apartment was quite new; a family had purchased the house the previous year and relied on the rent.

She sat on a stool watching the street through the window, her foot absently tapping against the wall. Suddenly, the plaster gave way.

Peeking into the hole, she discovered a yellowed letter from a boy her age. He'd lived in the attic, too, but he'd been hiding.

Olympian

Running the race at noon would be a challenge, but challenges were nothing new. He'd trained half his life for this. The eyes of people watching around the world were upon him.

He'd woken at 7, eaten the correct foods, hydrated properly, and arrived in plenty of time to stretch and warm up. He hadn't expected a race delay due to a scheduling snafu, but adapting was nothing new either.

The sun baked the track. He wiped the sweat sliding towards his eyes.

This was his moment. Just one thing left: re-check the prosthetic that served as his left leg.

Imagine

The tourists sat at a table by the sea, chatting over pretty, pink drinks. She heard one of them say, "I imagine myself sailing out on that yacht, not on the small boat we rented."

She understood imagining. When she was young, her mother helped her imagine that bread was something more. "Think of it as a round vanilla cake," her mother said. They each ate a piece, then described how it tasted.

That night, after a long day of work, she stood at the door of the small house she'd purchased.

"I don't have to imagine anymore," she said.

Waterfall

She'd made a mistake, so she took a walk. The path led to a waterfall washing the side of a small boulder cliff. The water flowed strongest after a long, cold winter.

As her boots sunk into mud, the water plunged into a waiting pool, then spun around smooth-sided rocks. Finally, it settled into a slim winding brook that bubbled past her feet.

Her life felt like that water: plunging, spinning…settling.

Where did the brook go? She didn't know. But she had to admit that the fall was quite spectacular, and *the water flowed strongest after a long, cold winter.*

Sandcastle

The waves swept the boy's sandcastle away. Tears pricked at his eyes as the ocean rolled back and forth, to and from the shore.

A gray-bearded man strolling by saw the boy, whose mother sat watching on a beach chair nearby.

"What's the matter?" asked the man.

"My sandcastle is gone," cried the boy.

"Why did you build it?" the man asked.

"I like building things. It's fun."

"Has that changed?" the man asked.

The boy thought for a moment. "No."

"Then what is important is not lost; it's inside you. Think what fun it will be to build another!"

Nell

Nell spied them in an open dumpster on her way home from school. They were lying on top of a heap of garbage bags.

On the bus, she cradled them carefully on her lap. Then she walked the three blocks to their brick apartment building and rode the creaky elevator up to the 18th floor. She unlocked the door and snuck into the bedroom she shared with her grandmother.

Later, her grandmother gasped when she entered the room.

"They're solar," Nell explained. "Our bill won't go up."

Her grandmother beamed. Dripping with fairy lights, their room could cradle new dreams.

Finally

Five years had passed since he left. So many tears, so many sad songs.

That morning he'd showered, grabbed his backpack, and headed back to his apartment to finish packing. "I'll call you when I get there, probably next week," he said after kissing her good-bye.

He never called. One letter four weeks later, then silence.

She waited nervously at the picnic table, the western sky stretching over the mountains.

When she saw him walking towards her, she was surprised. He was just a normal man. She didn't feel much at all.

"Hi," she said pleasantly, finally free of him.

Show and Tell

On "Show and Tell" day, the children examined each other's offerings before class.

"This is my father's medal," said one boy. The children—rightfully—ooo'd and ahhh'd.

"I have a photo from Ireland," said another.

"What have you got, Ava?" said one girl, pointing at Ava's box. "That's just rocks and things. You're supposed to bring something interesting."

A few children chuckled. Ava had always been a little different.

When the time came to show their items, Ava stood in front and took a shiny white pebble from her box.

"This is the first gift the crows brought," she said.

Her Voice

Lucy understood she was in the hospital, but she couldn't open her eyes. She vaguely remembered being admitted. She didn't want to die.

"Listen to the angel," her mother's voice whispered. Her mother had been gone twenty years, so it was strange to hear her voice.

I don't want to, Lucy tried to respond. An angel would tell her to follow; if she did, she wouldn't wake up.

Her mother's voice: "Listen to the angel."

"Can you open your eyes?" a younger voice said. This voice was louder, more real.

Lucy's eyes fluttered open, and she saw the R.N. badge.

Dark Night

The old coat was too thin. Snow fell hard. Huddled behind a dumpster, he was barely protected from the wind.

Holiday lights twinkled in the windows of the apartment block. He remembered those days — the bank where he'd worked, decorating a Christmas tree with a woman he'd adored.

How had he come to this?

He wanted to give up, but a whimper roused him. He patted Truman's head. For his dog, he couldn't give up. Somehow his wretched heart could still love.

Love. It was what prompted the young couple to approach him and, with kind words, offer to help.

The Airport

The delay was almost unbearable. He'd spent hours sitting bored at the crowded gate, fiddling with his phone, tugging his carry-on into a newspaper shop, staring at the screen showing canceled departures.

An announcement over the PA system elicited frustrated groans.

He wandered into a restaurant, but the bar stools were all taken.

"Hey!" called a voice from a round table with a vacant seat.

A group of travelers sat with suitcases by their sides and welcoming smiles on their faces. Hesitant, he approached them.

"Sit down," a woman said, patting the empty chair. "We're strangers becoming friends. Join us."

Her Time

Despite what people thought, she didn't mind. For most of the year she was stuck in a room at the back of the house. Out here, she could see the trees and sky.

Bundled up neighbors wandered by. Some walked alone, others in pairs. Occasionally a dog arrived to sniff the faded grass or venture onto the yard to explore the rhododendrons.

White ruffled sleeves peeked from her purple shawl. Despite the sparkling snow, she felt no cold.

At night, she slowly waved her candle back and forth. "How beautiful," said one passer-by, pointing at the doll in the window.

PART

Five:

LIFE

Her Smile

Whenever they saw her running along the bike path, they wondered about her smile.

She smiled as she entered the park, and later while gasping for breath. She smiled when the day was sunny and warm; she smiled when it was cold and wet.

Once, she smiled while wiping snow off her windbreaker after she'd slipped on hard winter ice.

"Is she crazy?" Regina asked her friend, eyebrows raised.

Her friend shrugged.

They didn't know she once lay in a hospital bed while her parents gripped her hands, fighting tears. The doctor had just declared she might never walk again.

Rock On

A grin spread across Ella's face.

Eyes sparkling, she turned to Renee, seated next to her. Renee glanced across the table at Evelyn, and Evelyn looked excitedly at Mengying.

This was their song!

They kicked off their shoes, one by one, and stood up. Grasping hands, laughing heartily, they headed to the dance floor. Their friends would stare, but they didn't mind. *This was their song.*

Throwing up their hands, they swung their hair and shook their booty. The bouncy beat drove them into a frenzy of fun.

Why not? Ella thought. *Why shouldn't we dance at my granddaughter's wedding?*

Old Bones

These days, it was difficult to climb into bed. She shifted slowly and carefully, her old bones hurting. It took time to find a comfortable position, to settle into the Land of Nod.

When her eyes closed, she envisioned the world when she was young. She remembered it all. She could feel herself moving with graceful ease, running on strong legs. Back then, running was second nature.

After a while she drifted into the Land of Dreams, where she moved like a winged angel.

While she was dreaming, her crooked legs became restless. Her ears pricked; her long tail twitched.

Carousel of Happiness™

In summer, the day would have been warm and sun-drenched; December led to a different story.

Hoping to hike, they'd packed water, snacks, and first aid kits. Rain ruined their plans.

The quirky mountain town offered a coffee shop, pizza, and a store selling crystals. A round building bore a sign: "Carousel." Normally they wouldn't have bothered, but the rain drove them in.

The animals were sensational: a camel, moose, elephant, giraffe, and many more, all hand-carved by a Vietnam veteran.

Joyful, surprised, they danced in December, around, up, and down, while music streamed out of a Wurlitzer band organ.

An Act of Kindness

She was not a high school beauty - no cheerleader, no queen of the prom. Still, he'd liked her, and when they shared picnics and walks, he was nice.

Then the new girl moved in.

Now she was alone, waiting in the line to buy a ticket to the movie everyone wanted to see. She spotted them walking towards her and thought she'd be sick.

Behind her, the popular quarterback clowned with his buddies. She had helped him once with his homework for math. When her ex approached, the quarterback suddenly reached for her hand.

Her ex's expression was priceless.

The Lonely Path

She had hoped to see other people strolling along the path. The air was frigid, but the trees still displayed their autumn colors.

Usually at least a cyclist or a jogger passed by, but today she saw no one.

Disappointed, she sighed.

The sound of hooves clopping on frozen mud surprised her. Looking up, she saw a small red barn next to a corral. A thick brown horse ambled along the fence.

The horse accompanied her quietly, matching her step-to-step. Eventually, the fence blocked its way.

She stopped, and they locked eyes.

"Thank you," she said, knowing the horse understood.

Butterflies

She loved watching butterflies. Instead of flying from one place to another in a straight line, they floated like snowflakes tossed in the wind—up, down, left, right.

Two years had passed since she'd moved in. Her apartment was small, but certainly adequate. Familiar paintings and photographs hung on the walls. That helped.

She continued with her artwork, and the butterflies brought her joy. Their flight provoked endless fascination. She enjoyed seeing them land so gently on the flowers. Their colors were like kaleidoscopes on oscillating wings. Just dazzling.

Thankfully, art was both inside and outside. It redefined "assisted living."

Lunch

Ten dollars, fifteen. It wouldn't be enough.

He had come here every year since they were married on this date, even after she was gone. What they paid for lunch sixty years ago wouldn't buy a soda now.

The server arrived. Nervous, he cleared his throat. "I don't think I have—"

The server stopped him, patting his arm. "Don't worry, it's taken care of. Another customer." She smiled and cleared his plates.

Stunned, he looked around. The front door was closing behind a young woman carrying a baby. He had held the door open for her when he'd arrived.

Children's Books

She spotted a sign: "Children's Books."

Glancing at the hardcovers displayed on a table, she chose one about a feral cat who found a home. On a shelf, she found two books she remembered from childhood: one about a train, another that told the story of an orphaned fawn. The common thread: overcoming adversity.

Back home, she wrapped the books. Using a marker, she wrote five words on one.

The next morning, the little girl who lost everything in the fire felt a lump under her pillow at the shelter. Three wrapped presents! From whom?

"With Love, the Book Fairy."

UNITED WE STA

The Children

She'd never had a child of her own. Between health problems and the divorce, it just hadn't happened.

Now she taught students at a neighborhood school. She decorated her classroom with drawings, colorful letters, and a large inspirational quote. She showed the children maps of the world during geography and explained about sums during math. She laughed when her students laughed, and she grinned when they grinned. When they appeared to be tired or to have a problem, she helped.

These children were not hers. She never thought or pretended they were.

She simply left her own kind of legacy.

Syrup

Her favorite stuffed bear was named Syrup. She'd received him as a birthday present. Her mother had prepared pancakes for breakfast that day, and the syrup was sweet and brown, like her bear.

She loved Syrup. Syrup always smiled. On good days, he smiled. On hard days, he smiled. In the middle of dark nights while she dreamed life's dreams, Syrup smiled.

It was her birthday again, and she'd been celebrating with friends at a party. She climbed up the stairs, entered her room, and picked up Syrup. She hugged him.

"I'm sixty today, Syrup," she said, and he smiled.

After Six

Since he'd died, she hadn't left the house after six. That was when they'd walked the dog every night, enjoying an evening stroll around the neighborhood. Those walks had been one of life's small pleasures.

Alone, she couldn't face the falling light of dusk. So, the dog, after looking hopefully at his leash, settled for the backyard at six.

Sometimes she stared out the window in the front room and watched the sun set, quietly missing him.

One evening at six she went to the window and saw them—a small group of neighbors at her door, dogs in tow.

Monica

Monica refused to go to school. Fifth grade was painful enough in their last town; she'd always felt strange being the only student in a wheelchair.

Monica's mother contacted the school principal and explained. The principal, concerned, then spoke to Ms. Beckman.

Ms. Beckman wasn't having it. No child would feel uncomfortable in *her* class.

Monica reluctantly agreed to go to school the next day. She felt nervous as her mom pushed her wheelchair through the classroom door.

Then, she stared in shock.

A "WELCOME MONICA" banner hung on the wall, and every applauding child sat in a borrowed wheelchair.

The Park

He touched her hand. She sat next to him on the bench, watching the children.

Some swung on the swing set, pushed by a parent and squealing with delight. Others climbed the moon-shaped monkey bars, hanging on as hard as they could before the inevitable fall.

It *was* fall. Orange and yellow leaves hung on the maple trees. Some fluttered towards the ground, drifting on the breeze.

He glanced at her. He knew what they saw: an elderly woman with white hair and furrowed skin.

But he saw the young girl she once was, laughing and swinging in the park.

Her Song

Where were you yesterday?

Thanks to hard work, Valeria's family had moved to the lovely town. Now she was part of an online parents' group.

I was at work, then I dropped off my song at soccer, she wrote.

Laughing emojis appeared. Valeria felt confused.

You mean "son," not "song."

Valeria didn't type well in English. Embarrassed, she added her own laughing emoji to feel part of the group.

That afternoon, she again drove Mattheo to soccer practice. As she watched him race happily towards his teammates, she wondered if her heart might burst.

He IS my song, she thought.

He Wanted to Tell Her

"I love you," she said.

He stared at her, unsure how to respond. For a year, he had done everything he could to express how he felt.

"I love you so much," she said. Then she hugged him.

Without knowing how to answer — how to say the words — he could do nothing but remain still. Her arms felt warm around his neck. Tears spilled down her cheek, damp against his own.

No matter what happened, he would stay by her side. She would never be alone. How he *wanted* to tell her.

He licked her face and wagged his tail.

Birth Day

To Do:

1. Order a gift for my gorgeous girl

2. Buy butter, balloons, flour, and frosting

3. Bake a monster-decorated cake (family joke)

4. Organize and send email invitations

5. Clean, mop, dust

6. Decorate

Were party games "de rigueur" these days? Polly didn't know, but she could certainly do some research. Silly, perhaps, but why not have some fun? Her daughter's friends might enjoy silly games.

Polly doodled on the calendar, remembering the ambulance, the scare, the relief when all was well.

She smiled. She'd always remember her daughter's first day, even if Violet would soon be forty.

Stunning

She was stunning. Her smile almost stung; her hair sparkled like diamonds under the lamp above the bar. He looked away, embarrassed. She was out of his league.

Anyway, he didn't expect to meet someone here. He was lonely, yes, but only because Fridays had been their date night. The din of a dive bar was all he needed.

Next to him, a woman sat with friends. She was relatively plain, and he hadn't noticed her. When her coat dropped to the floor, he politely picked it up. She thanked him, and the shyness in her smile snatched his heart.

Steadfast

She assumed no one cared. Steadfast for years, she'd spent her life supplying necessities. She didn't mind; it was her lot. Rooted in this place, it was reassuring to know and grow here.

Through the years, they flocked to her for refuge. She gave; they took what they needed. If they wanted to stay, she offered shelter.

Two friends lived next door. Their company provided cheer through the hot summer days and cold winter nights. When she waved, they waved back.

She assumed no one cared, but she was wrong. The family who lived in the house loved their tree.

Pink Umbrellas

The rain started while they sat in a café drinking coffee. Forty years had passed since they'd last seen each other.

Hands above their heads, they raced across the square and ducked into a pharmacy to buy cheap umbrellas. Pointing and giggling, they purchased what looked like pink parasols. Then they stepped back outside, almost skipping down the street.

The thick clouds parted to reveal a lazy sun. The rain stopped. They shook the pink umbrellas and closed them up.

At the station, Margaret smiled. "We were teenagers again."

Fran hugged her old friend. "We were free again," she said.

Classic Rock

He wasn't crazy. He'd rented a small trailer and loaded it up with the furniture his daughter wanted for her apartment. Now he was driving across two states to deliver it. Maybe he *was* crazy.

He found some classic rock on the radio, and a familiar tune clanged into the car.

His fingers started tapping on the steering wheel. He opened the window and let the wind blow what was left of his hair. Bopping his head back and forth, he started singing.

Just like that he was 18 again, flying down the road towards his first days of freedom.

Sophie

Every child was different. They knew this; they'd raised two girls and a boy after getting married very young.

They had been lucky after a rough start; love grew, and their marriage became comfortable. Financial struggles faded. He worked. She worked. Over dinner, they chuckled and chatted about grown children. Really, nothing was missing.

The fourth, Sophie, was an unexpected addition.

He admittedly hadn't been thrilled about number four.

Now, she smiled when he coddled the new baby. Usually remote, he melted when he saw her. The house was filled with toys again.

Every child was different. This one barked.

The Survivor's Daughter

When you see a white bird, you will know I am with you, her father's voice said.

She woke up.

She still hadn't processed his life or his loss. Searching for answers only led to more questions. Those questions never had answers.

Now, she was on another "wild goose chase." She looked up white birds: goose (of course), great egret, snowy owl, white ibis. Not likely in the city. Sighing, she stepped outside to fill the feeders.

When it landed on the fence, she laughed.

Was it a coincidence that today a white pigeon appeared?

Life: just question after question.

Acknowledgments

Many people helped along the road to the publication of this book, but there are a few people whose efforts it is important to recognize here. First, I'd like to thank Joshua Adams, owner and publisher of Huntsville Independent Press, for his hard work and his unwavering support of this manuscript from the day he read it.

I'd also like to thank the editors of the literary journals that published one or more of these stories before they appeared in the book.

I am so grateful to Anya Lauchlan, whose gorgeous artwork and illustrations grace these pages. Thanks also to Alison Stone, whose poetry drafts always inspire me to keep writing, and to the Carousel of Happiness™ for allowing me to use the real name of their beautiful carousel in Nederland, Colorado, after it inspired me to write a fictional tiny story.

Finally, I am grateful to Lori Groudas, Joan Schweighardt, and Cindy Zelman for reading portions of this manuscript early on and/or helping me shape Soul to Soul into its final version.

Thank you.

– Faye Rapoport DesPres

Previously Published Work

"By the Sea" first appeared in *The Dribble Drabble Review*, Spring 2022, Issue V. It later won a Best Microfiction 2023 award and was anthologized in *Best Microfiction 2023*.

"Dark Night" first appeared in *Friday Flash Fiction*, April 12, 2021.

"Darkness" first appeared in *Friday Flash Fiction*, Dec. 2, 2021.

"Generations" first appeared in *The Centifictionist*, Spring/Summer 2022 Issue.

"Party Clown," first appeared in *The Drabble*, March 2022.

"The Giver" first appeared in *Story in 100 Words*, Feb. 9, 2022.

"The Last Gift" first appeared in *Friday Flash Fiction, Dec. 13, 2021.*

"The Place" first appeared in *The Centifictionist*, Spring/Summer 2022 Issue.

About the Illustrator

Anya Lauchlan, a distinguished scholar with a Master's degree in Art & Publishing Design, boasts an illustrious lineage of artistic tutelage, having been trained under the watchful eye of a direct disciple of the visionary Marc Chagall. Embracing the rich tapestry of the esteemed School of Paris art movement, Lauchlan's captivating creations have found their way onto the global stage,  gracing prestigious exhibitions across the world. A mere glimpse into her awe-inspiring portfolio at anyalauchlan.com will unveil a treasure trove of visual wonders. Moreover, her profound artistic prowess extends beyond the realms of canvas, as she has lent her talents to the realm of literature, illustrating a myriad of captivating books for European publishers. It is with great honor that Huntsville Independent Press presents her delightful illustrations in Faye's brilliant collection of stories.

About the Author

Faye Rapoport DesPres is an award-winning journalist and the author of five books, including the memoir-in-essays *Message From a Blue Jay* (2014) and three children's books: *Little White the Feral Cat Who Found a Home* (2018), *Tribbs: The Very Handsome Cat* (2020), and *Frazier: The Very Special Cat* (2021). Her fiction, creative nonfiction, and poetry have appeared in a variety of literary journals, including *Ascent, Bending Genres, Connotation Press: An Online Artifact, The Centifictionist* and *The Dribble Drabble Review*. One of her stories, "By the Sea," won a Best Microfiction 2023 award. Faye earned her MFA at the Solstice Creative Writing Program and has taught writing at Framingham State University and Lasell University, as well as in online classes for children. An outdoors lover who advocates for animals and the environment, she donates a portion of the proceeds from her children's books to non-profit animal rescue organizations. Faye lives in Massachusetts with her husband, Jean-Paul Des Pres, and their rescued cats.

www.ingramcontent.com/pod-product-compliance
Lightning Source LLC
Chambersburg PA
CBHW041738300726
48978CB00006B/151